S0-EXM-141

PLEASE RETURN TO
TIMOTHY CHRISTIAN SCHOOL
2008 Ethel Road
Piscataway, NJ 08854

FOOTBALL LEGENDS

Troy Aikman

Terry Bradshaw

Jim Brown

John Elway

Brett Favre

Michael Irvin

Vince Lombardi

John Madden

Dan Marino

Joe Montana

Joe Namath

Walter Payton

Jerry Rice

Barry Sanders

Deion Sanders

Emmitt Smith

Lawrence Taylor

Steve Young

CHELSEA HOUSE PUBLISHERS

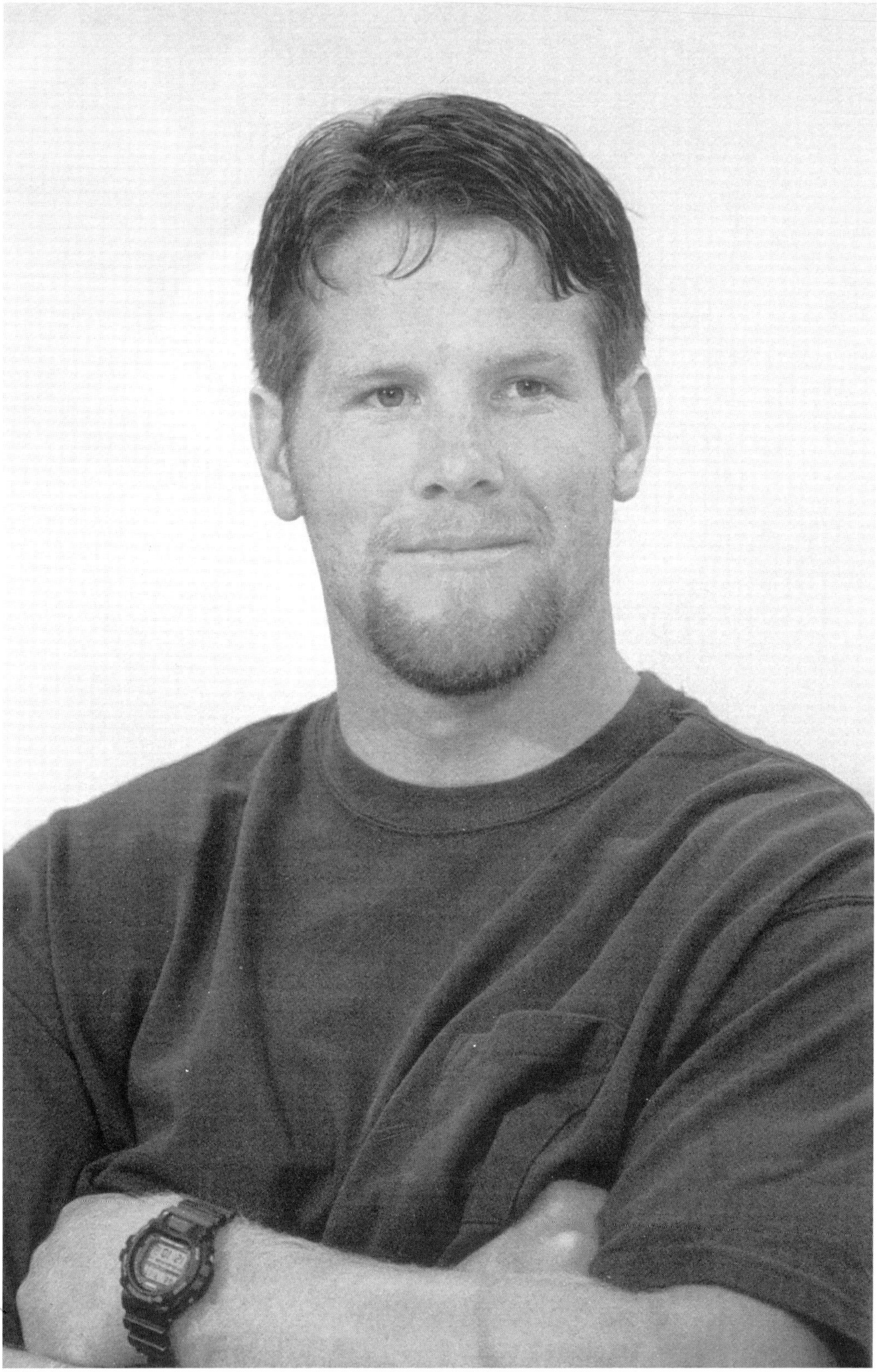

FOOTBALL LEGENDS

BRETT FAVRE

Martin J. Mooney

*Introduction by
Chuck Noll*

The inclusion of this book in
the Timothy Christian School
library does not constitute an
agreement with the material
contained in it.

CHELSEA HOUSE PUBLISHERS
Philadelphia

Produced by Daniel Bial and Associates
New York, New York

Picture research by Alan Gottlieb
Cover illustration by Bill Vann

© 1997, 1999 by Chelsea House Publishers, a division of Main Line Book Co.
All rights reserved. Printed and bound in the United States of America.

3 5 7 9 8 6 4 2

Library of Congress Cataloging-in-Publication Data

Mooney, Martin J.
    Brett Favre / Martin J. Mooney.
      p. cm.—(Football Legends)
    Includes bibliographical references (p.) and index.
    Summary: Describes the life of the Green Bay Packers star quarterback
who has gained fame as a top passer in the game.
    ISBN 0-7910-4396-7 (hardcover)
    1. Favre, Brett—Juvenile literature. 2. Quarterback (Football)—United States—
    Biography—Juvenile literature. 3. Green Bay Packers (Football team)—Juvenile
    literature. [1. Favre, Brett. 2. Football players.] I. Title. II. Series.
GV939.F29M66 1997
796.332'092—dc21
[B]   97-14960
                                                                               CIP
                                                                                AC

CONTENTS

A Winning Attitude   6
Chuck Noll

CHAPTER 1
A Perfect Day   9

CHAPTER 2
Quarterback from "The Kill"   13

CHAPTER 3
Making the Big Time   23

CHAPTER 4
"Country" Riding High   31

CHAPTER 5
Putting It All Together   41

CHAPTER 6
The Road to New Orleans   55

Statistics   61
Chronology   62
Further Reading   63
Index   64

A Winning Attitude

Chuck Noll

Don't ever fall into the trap of believing, "I could never do that. And I won't even try—I don't want to embarrass myself." After all, most top athletes had no idea what they could accomplish when they were young. A secret to the success of every star quarterback and sure-handed receiver is that they tried. If they had not tried, if they had not persevered, they would never have discovered how far they could go and how much they could achieve.

You can learn about trying hard and overcoming challenges by being a sports fan. Or you can take part in organized sports at any level, in any capacity. The student messenger at my high school is now president of a university. A reserve ballplayer who got very little playing time in high school now owns a very successful business. Both of them benefited by the lesson of perseverance that sports offers. The main point is that you don't have to be a Hall of Fame athlete to reap the benefits of participating in sports.

In math class, I learned that the whole is equal to the sum of its parts. But that is not always the case when you are dealing with people. Sports has taught me that the whole is either greater than or less than the sum of its parts, depending on how well the parts work together. And how the parts work together depends on how they really understand the concept of teamwork.

Most people believe that teamwork is a fifty-fifty proposition. But true teamwork is seldom, if ever, fifty-fifty. Teamwork is *whatever it takes to get the job done.* There is no time for the measurement of contributions, no time for anything but concentrating on your job.

One year, my Pittsburgh Steelers were playing the Houston Oilers in the Astrodome late in the season, with the division championship on the line. Our offensive line was hard hit by the flu, our starting quarterback was out with an injury, and we were having difficulty making a first down. There was tremendous pressure on our defense to perform well—and they rose to the occasion. If the players on the defensive unit had been measuring their contribution against the offense's contribution, they would have given up and gone home. Instead, with a "whatever it takes" attitude, they increased their level of concentration and performance, forced turnovers, and got the ball into field goal range for our offense. Thanks to our defense's winning attitude, we came away with a victory.

Believing in doing whatever it takes to get the job done is what separates a successful person from someone who is not as successful. Nobody can give you this winning outlook; you have to develop it. And I know from experience that it can be learned and developed on the playing field.

My favorite people on the football field have always been offensive linemen and defensive backs. I say this because it takes special people to perform well in jobs in which there is little public recognition when they are doing things right but are thrust into the spotlight as soon as they make a mistake. That is exactly what happens to a lineman whose man sacks the quarterback or a defensive back who lets his receiver catch a touchdown pass. They know the importance of being part of a group that believes in teamwork and does not point fingers at one another.

Sports can be a learning situation as much as it can be fun. And that's why I say, "Get involved, Participate."

CHUCK NOLL, the Pittsburgh Steelers head coach from 1969-1991, led his team to four Super Bowl victories—the most by any coach. Widely respected as an innovator on both offense and defense, Noll was inducted into the Pro Football Hall of Fame in 1993.

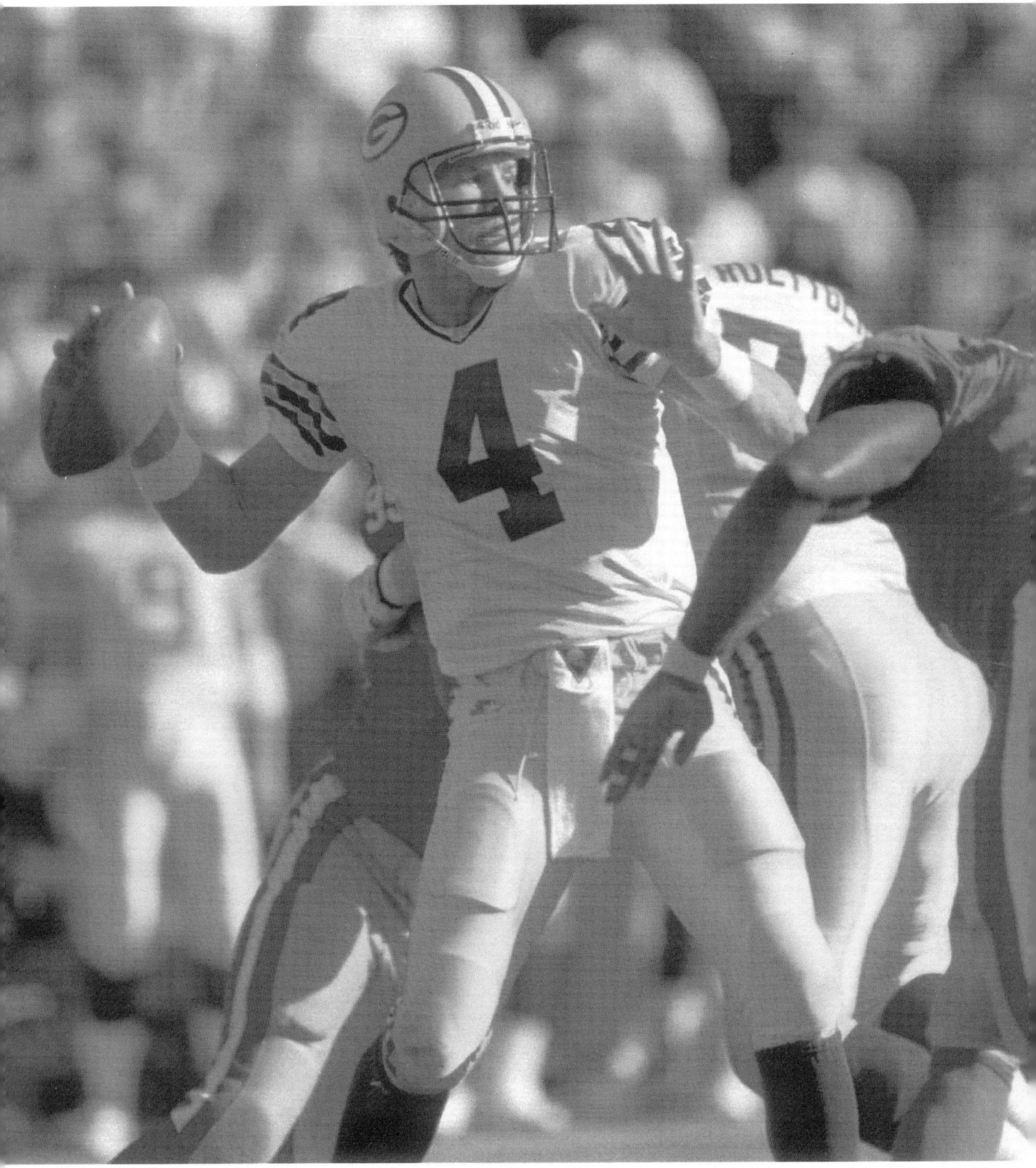

1
A PERFECT DAY

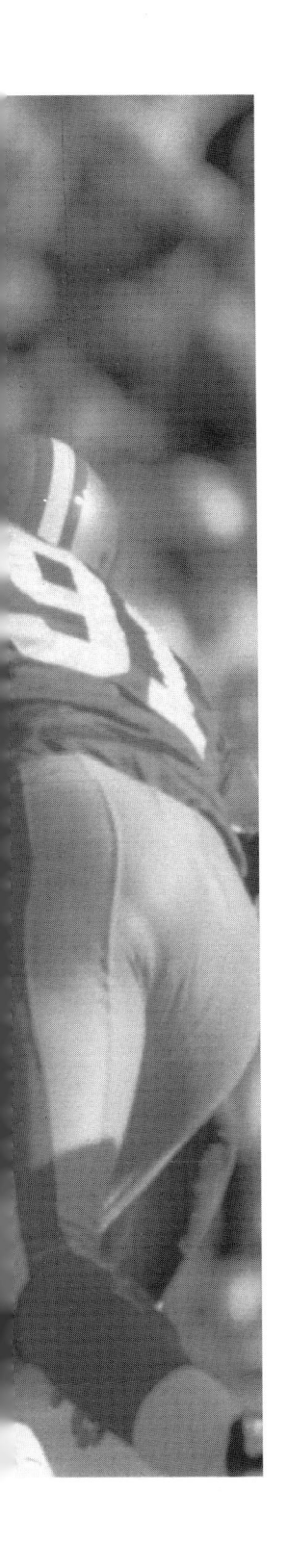

Things were going well for Brett Favre the first week in January 1996. On New Year's Eve, he led his Green Bay Packers to victory in the first round of the playoffs against the Atlanta Falcons. Three days later, he was named the National Football League's Most Valuable Player, and on January 6, he had a chance to make history against the defending Super Bowl Champions, the San Francisco 49ers.

Beating the 49ers would not be easy. This was a team that had won a record five Super Bowls. It boasted one of the most powerful offenses in NFL history, featuring 1994 MVP quarterback Steve Young and future Hall of Famer Jerry Rice catching passes.

The Packers were no "Cinderella" team, making the playoffs by getting lucky and playing way above their heads. Green Bay finished the 1995

Brett Favre drops back to pass under pressure from Alfred Williams during the NFC playoff game against the San Francisco 49ers.

regular season with an 11-5 record and won the NFC's tough Central Division. Brett Favre was the NFL's number-one-ranked passer in 1995, throwing for more than 4,400 yards and almost 40 touchdowns. While his flashy style and off-the-field behavior might have rubbed some people the wrong way, no one could argue with the results he posted. With only five years in the league, the 26-year-old from Mississippi had helped to put Green Bay back on the map.

The game started off poorly for the visiting Packers. On their first possession, Green Bay moved the ball 48 yards upfield before being stopped at the 49er 29 yardline. However, with eight minutes left in the quarter, the 49ers blocked a 46-yard field goal attempt by Chris Jacke. This would be one of the few mistakes the Packers made all afternoon.

The next play after the blocked field goal would serve notice to the 49ers that this was going to be a long day. San Francisco quarterback Steve Young threw a screen pass to Adam Walker, who was hit so hard by Green Bay linebacker Wayne Simmons that he fumbled the ball—right into the waiting arms of cornerback Craig Newsome, who scampered 31 yards into the end zone to give the Pack an early 7-0 lead.

On the next possession, Brett needed only three passes to give the visitors from Wisconsin a 14-0 lead. The first play was a 35-yard gain to tight end Keith Jackson. The second was a perfect lob pass to Michael Brooks. And the third was a 3-yard strike, again to Jackson waiting by himself in the end zone. The Niners were on the ropes and there still was six minutes left to play in the first quarter.

Before the half ended, Brett hooked up with

one of his favorite receivers—and good friends—Mark Chmura, for a 13-yard touchdown strike. Going into the locker room with a 21-0 lead might have given some players a feeling that the game was over, but the Packers knew better. The San Francisco 49ers were world champions and would not just lie down and die. "When you're up 21-0 on most teams," tight end Keith Jackson said, "you're glad. But against the 49ers, you get nervous." The offense had given the Packers a good lead in the first half, but in the second half it was up to the defense to preserve it.

On the line of scrimmage, Reggie White put constant pressure on Steve Young all day, giving the 49ers quarterback little time to throw. In addition, linebackers Wayne Simmons and Fred Strickland and strong safety LeRoy Butler blitzed Young often, causing one fumble and two interceptions.

As for Brett Favre, this was the game that showed the whole country who the best young quarterback in football was. In front of a national television audience, Brett completed 22 out of 28 passes—including 15 of his first 16—for 299 yards, 2 touchdowns, and 0 interceptions. The day went so well for Brett that even when he stumbled to his knees on one play, he was able to quickly get up and fire a strike to an open Keith Jackson. Green Bay had the engine running on all cylinders that day in San Francisco and won 27-17.

Although the Packers would lose their next game to the Dallas Cowboys, Brett Favre and Co. had just served notice that they were heir apparents to the crown.

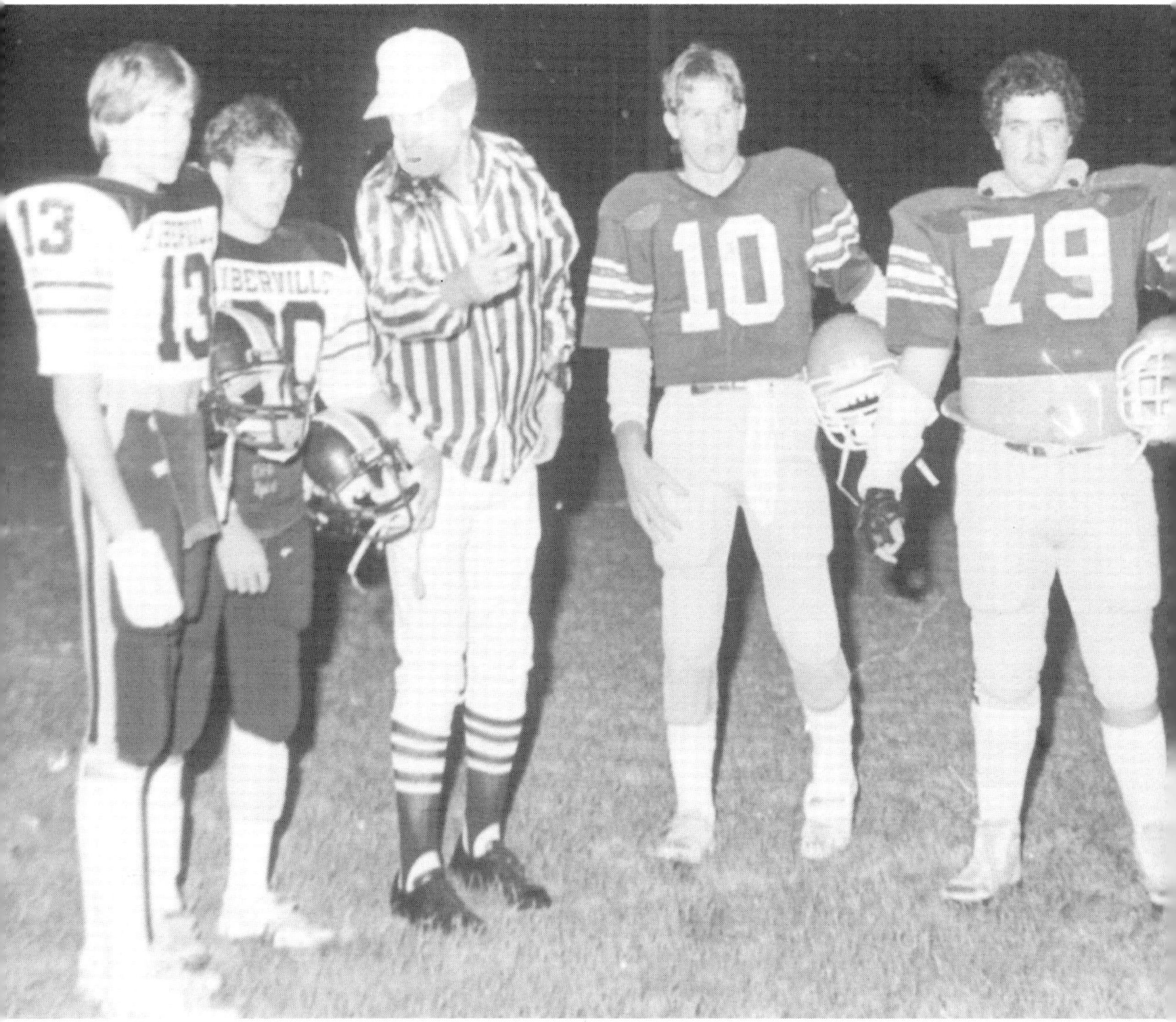
13
13
10
79

2
A QUARTERBACK FROM "THE KILL"

Brett Favre grew up in the small town of Kiln, Mississippi. Lying eight miles north of the Gulf of Mexico, the town is locally known as "the Kill." It is a place where everybody knows everybody else; where people make a living in the various heavy manufacturing plants in Hancock County or on the shrimping and fishing boats on the coast; where for most people, a good time is a bucket of crawdads, a cold drink, and telling stories late into a warm summer night.

Brett Favre is the second oldest child of Irvin and Bonita Favre, who both worked in the Hancock County school districts. Irvin was a teacher and a baseball and football coach and Bonita was a special education teacher at Hancock North Central High School. Brett's father was a standout pitcher at the University of Southern Mississippi in the 1960s. Brett would someday follow in his father's footsteps at USM, but not as a baseball player.

Brett Favre (number 10) wanted to be a quarterback since the fifth grade.

As a child, Brett was always big for his age and was always a good athlete, but when he started playing football, he was not quite sure what position he wanted to play. As a fifth grader, he went out for wide receiver. On one play, he landed on the football after catching a pass, which knocked the wind out of him. After regaining his breath, he told his father "I don't want to play wide receiver no more." That day Irvin put him at quarterback, and, as Brett told *Sport Magazine*, "I threw for two touchdowns and ran for two—I knew this was the position for me."

Growing up the son of the football coach might seem to be a tough position for Brett to be in, but he never looked at it that way. "It really wasn't because I saw my dad involved in football every day. Watching dad coach football, I idolized the guys playing for them, and I wanted to be the best."

One of the older players Brett looked up to was his brother Scott, who was a good athlete in his own right. (He also has a younger brother, Jeff, and a younger sister, Brandi.) When Brett was an eighth grader, he played baseball on the same team as Scott for Hancock North Central. Scott recalled that Brett's being on the team "rubbed some of the guys the wrong way, and I took up for him. Heck, he was there because he could do the job and some of them couldn't."

Maybe as an upstart eighth grader Brett rubbed some people the wrong way, but by the time he graduated, he had become one of the most successful athletes Hancock North Central had ever produced. One of the honors bestowed the family was their address. The street in front of the Favre house was named Irvin Farve [sic] Road in the early 1980s to honor

Favre was a standout athlete in high school. Here he shows off a jump pass—a style he still uses sometimes in the pros.

the local football coach. Actually, the street is just a dirt road and the Favres are the only people who live on it. Brett's grandmother, Izella French, lives just up the road.

Brett's room remains largely the way it was when he grew up there. It is decorated with posters of Joe Montana and Charles Barkley, a picture of legendary University of Alabama football coach Bear Bryant, college and pro team pennants, trophies, awards, and medals. One of Brett's prize possessions is a 1982 Sugar Bowl program signed by Dan Marino, the great Miami Dolphin quarterback. Brett lived in this room throughout high school and college and even into his pro career. Early on with the Green Bay Packers, Brett was asked why he still lived at home. "Well," he said "I could be other places, but I can't think of one I'd rather be."

When the time came to choose a college, Brett

was recruited heavily by his father's alma mater, the University of Southern Mississippi, in Hattiesburg. USM wanted him, and that is where he decided to attend. Although the school is fairly big—the student population is about 11,000—it does not have the great football reputation of its rivals, such as Alabama, Georgia, or even Ole Miss. However, the school has produced some very good players who have gone on to the pros. In the 1980s running back Sammy Winder of the Denver Broncos and Louis Lipps of the Pittsburgh Steelers were stars at USM. Probably the best player Southern Miss ever produced was the All-Pro punter for the Oakland Raiders, Ray Guy. He helped the Raiders to two Super Bowl championships and is now in the Pro Football Hall of Fame. So, while Brett did not attend a football "factory," he did attend a school that would allow him to grow as both a student and football player.

Irvin Favre was Brett's football coach. He and Bonita stand in front of their house in Kiln, Mississippi.

Coming out of high school, Brett was big and fast enough to play a number of positions. He had played quarterback and defensive back in high school, and some coaches even thought that with his size—6'3", 195 pounds—he might even play somewhere on the line. However, when the offensive coaches saw him throw two touchdown passes against the number-one defense in a preseason scrimmage, they knew he would play quarterback.

Brett did not play right away, of course. Quar-

A Quarterback from "The Kill"

terback is the most demanding position on the football field. The person playing that position has to know every offensive play inside and out. He has to know what he is supposed to do, what the line is supposed to do, and what his receivers are supposed to do. Not only does he have to know all of this, but he must also make changes in the blink of an eye if the defense changes. Learning the position takes time, and even the great ones have to wait their turn. Although Brett practiced with the team his first year, he never appeared in a game. In order to learn his position he "red-shirted" his first year, which means that he could not play in games, but would be eligible to play the following four years. This experience proved valuable for the years ahead.

The following season, Brett still had to battle for playing time. As the season began, he was the third string quarterback, but by the second game, he had found his way onto the field. Brett came off the bench in the second half against Tulane University with his team down 24-17. He threw two touchdown passes to lead Southern Mississippi to an exciting come-from-behind victory. He would only miss one more game over the course of the next four years for the Golden Eagles.

That first year was a terrific one for the young man from Kiln. Brett completed 79 of 194 passes for 1264 yards, ran for 169 yards, and scored 1 touchdown himself. He led the team to victories over Tulane, East Carolina, Louisville, and Southwestern Louisiana. He also threw for a school record 14 touchdowns. The following year, the offense was revamped to showcase his talents even more.

When the 1988 season rolled around, Brett and the Eagles were ready to soar. In his successful sophomore season, Brett set a new single season passing record for USM, tossing for 2,271 yards. He became the first passer in Golden Eagle history to pass for more than 300 yards in one game with a 301-yard performance against East Carolina. He was intercepted only five times all season out of 319 attempts, the lowest ratio among the nation's top 50 quarterbacks. He also broke his own record for touchdown passes in a season with 16. Finally, Brett led the Eagles to a 10-2 record, one of their most successful seasons in years. This led to a berth in the Independence Bowl, where USM beat the University of Texas at El Paso 38-13, and Brett threw for 157 yards and 1 touchdown. For his performance, Brett was named the Independence Bowl Offensive Player of the Year.

Not content to rest on his laurels, Brett came back the next year determined to be a better player and did just that. To start the year, in a game that gave Brett national attention, the Golden Eagles defeated the national powerhouse Florida State Seminoles. Brett threw for 282 yards and 2 touchdown passes against the Seminoles and their star defensive back, Deion Sanders. In 1989, Brett broke his own record for passing yardage in a season with 2,588. He also set records for most passes completed in a season (206) and most yards in a single game with 345 against Memphis State.

At the end of the first three years of the Favre Era at Southern Mississippi, everyone, including Brett, was looking forward to his final season with the Eagles. He had done so many great things to this point, many people anticipated

A Quarterback from "The Kill"

1990 to be his best season yet, but it was almost a disaster.

On July 15, 1990, at 7:45 in the evening, Brett was traveling to his home in Kiln on a dark back-woods road. His brother Scott and Southern Mississippi linebacker Keith Loescher were following behind when a car approached them in the opposite direction and did not dim its high beams. Momentarily blinded by the light, Brett lost control of his car and spun out on a sharp turn. The Nissan Maxima he was driving flipped over and landed on the passenger side next to a pine tree. Scott and Keith had to use a golf club to break the windshield and get Brett out of the vehicle. The accident happened about a mile from the Favre home.

In the accident, Brett wound up with lacerations, a cracked vertebra, and a concussion. Because he was wearing his seat belt, he managed to avoid more serious injuries. The most serious result of the crash was the operation in which doctors removed a 30-inch section of Brett's small intestine.

Before the surgery, doctors said Brett might not play until the middle of the season. That prediction left many wondering if he would come back at all.

In their first game of the 1990 season, the Eagles were without Brett at the helm for the first time since 1987. They struggled to beat Delta State, a Division II team. With nationally-ranked Georgia, Alabama, and Auburn on the

Favre broke numerous records as a sophomore at the University of Southern Mississippi.

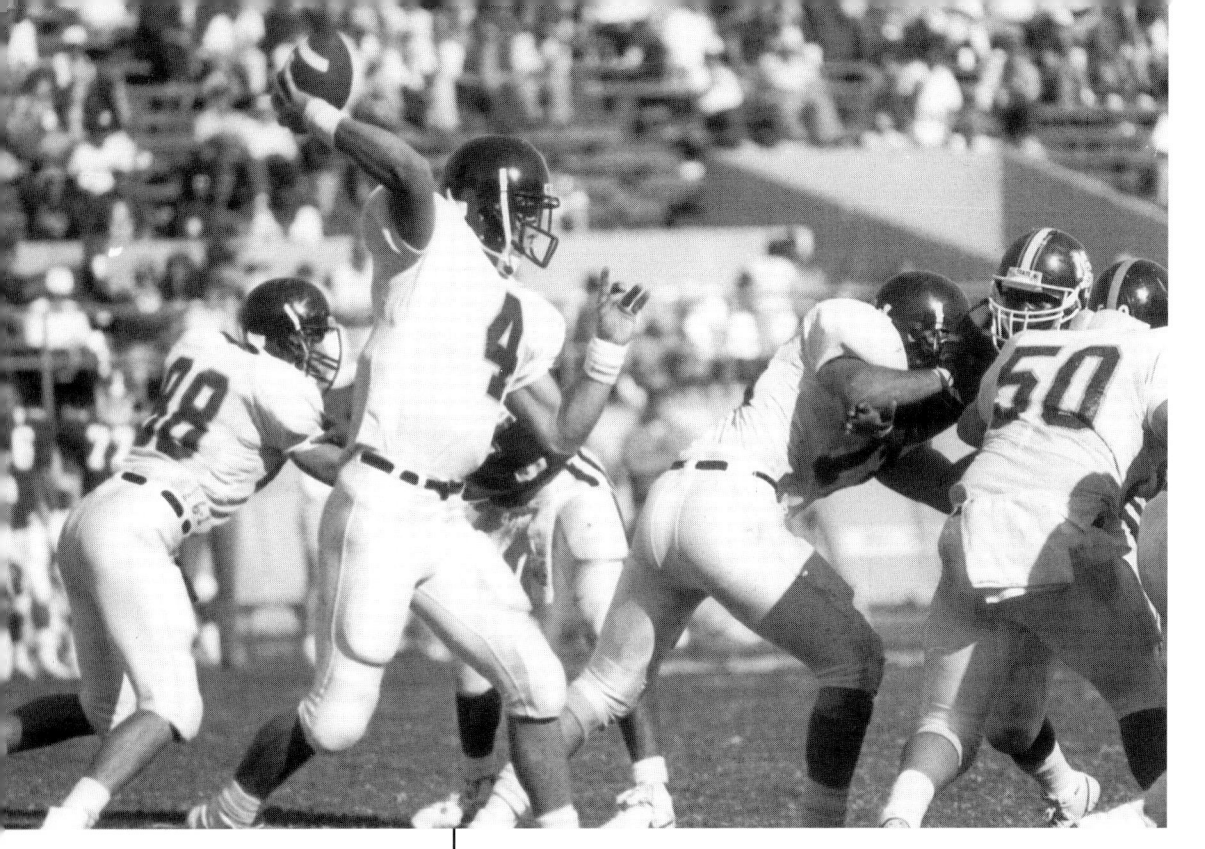

Favre had three great seasons playing for USM. But a car accident dampened his performance during his senior year.

schedule, the future for the Favre-less Eagles did not look bright.

But in the second week of the season, Brett Favre staged the biggest comeback of his career to that point. He returned to the lineup on September 8, only one month after major abdominal surgery, and six weeks after a disastrous car wreck, to lead the Eagles against 13th-ranked Alabama. Although he only completed 9 of 17 passes for 125 yards, his mere presence at the game lifted the Eagles high enough to beat the Crimson Tide, 27-24. A shocked Alabama head coach Gene Stallings told reporters after the game, "You can call it a miracle or a legend or whatever you want to. I just know that on that day, Brett Favre was larger than life."

Brett led the Eagles to a respectable 8-4 record that year, but never was able to fully make up for the time he lost because of the accident. Nevertheless, he played in the Senior Bowl and the East-West Shrine game where he received the notice of many pro scouts, including Ron Wolf, who was then a scout for the New York Jets, but who would be the man instrumental in bringing him to Green Bay.

Brett finished his career at Southern Mississippi as one of the most celebrated athletes ever to attend the Hattiesburg school. He owns just about every major passing record, but he will probably be remembered more for his leadership and his courage. The school retired his jersey, number 4, in 1993.

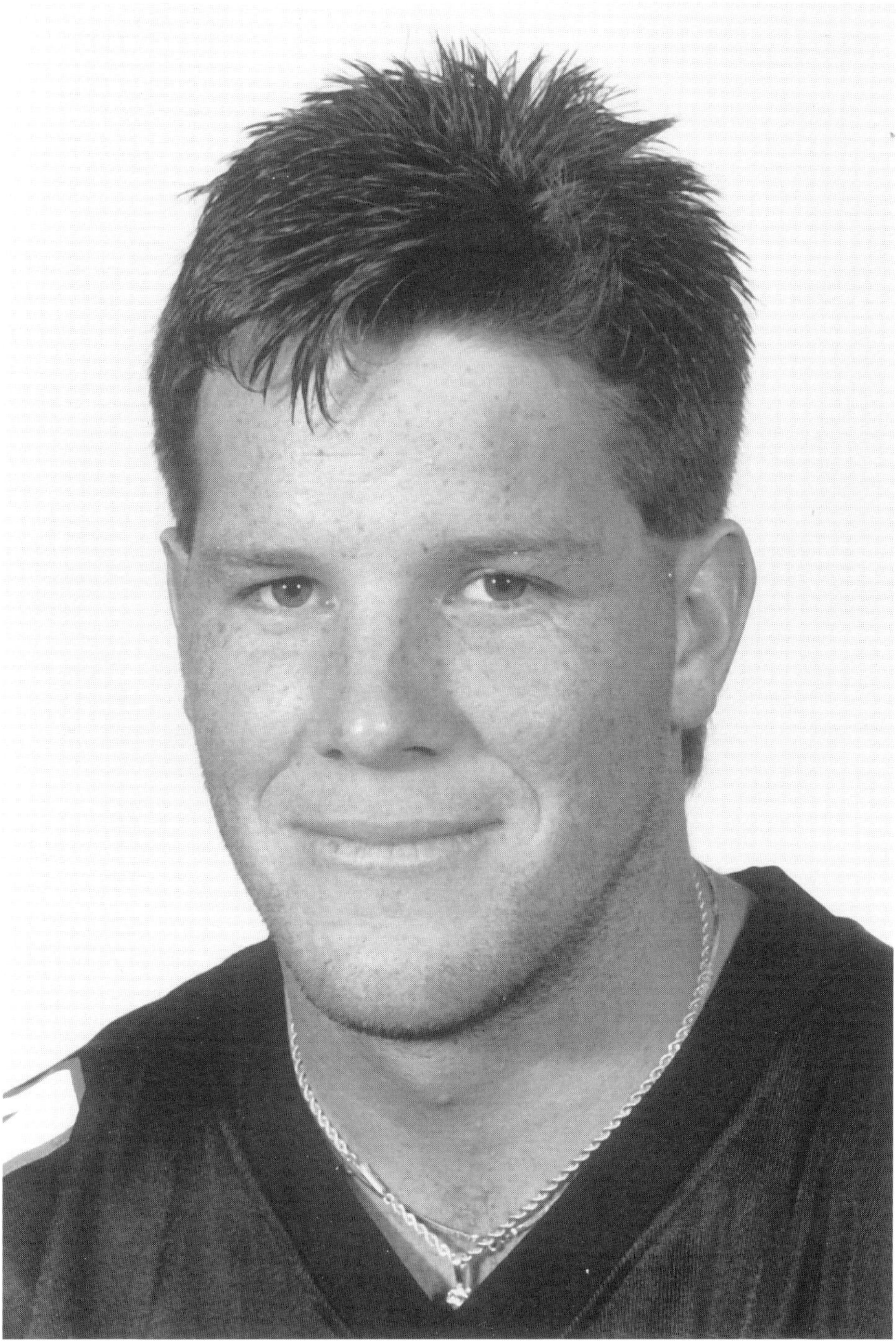

3
MAKING THE BIG TIME

Although Brett was able to complete his senior year at Southern Miss, he was not able to post the numbers that he had in his sophomore and junior years. It took him a while to get into shape and to shake off the effects of the car accident. As a result, Brett's stock as a professional prospect had gone down, and he was not chosen until the second round of the 1991 NFL draft by the Atlanta Falcons.

Brett was the 33rd pick overall in the draft and the third quarterback; USC's Todd Marinovich and San Diego State's Dan McGwire were drafted ahead of him. He reported to training camp one day before it began after signing a contract that would pay him $1.4 million for three years, with a signing bonus of $350,000.

In the 1991 season, Brett completed no passes in five attempts. Two of them were intercepted. Although Brett had achieved his dream

Favre was drafted by the Falcons. He saw almost no playing time as Atlanta's third-string quarterback.

by making it to the NFL, he was no longer the superstar he had been in college.

Even while Brett was riding the bench in Atlanta, factors were at work that would change his career in ways he never could have imagined. While playing in the East-West Shrine Game, an all-star game in college football, Brett caught the attention of Ron Wolf, a scout for the New York Jets. Wolf was very impressed with Brett's athletic ability but was even more taken with his take-charge attitude in the huddle and his overall leadership on the field.

In the 1991 draft, the Jets wanted to choose Brett. Unfortunately, they had no first-round pick and had to wait to see if they could nab him with their number seven pick in the second round. However, six picks into the second round, the Falcons chose Brett and the Jets had to settle for Browning Nagle, a quarterback from Louisville University.

The next season, Wolf signed on as the general manager of the Green Bay Packers. But he did not forget about the former Golden Eagle.

In 1991, the Falcons' starting quarterback, Chris Miller, led the team to the playoffs and was named to the Pro Bowl. Brett was a third-string quarterback with little chance of seeing action. It did not help that he was late for team meetings, stayed out late at night, did not study his plays, and was forever in Coach Jerry Glanville's doghouse. He even managed to miss the Falcons team picture. Although he set his alarm for 8:30 so he would not miss the picture session, he did not arrive until 11:00, long after the photos were taken. Brett was fined $1500 for his tardiness.

On February 10, 1992, Favre received unusually good news. The Green Bay Packers had acquired him in exchange for a first-round draft pick. By all accounts, people thought that Green Bay's general manager, Ron Wolf, was crazy. Who would trade a first-round draft pick for a third-string quarterback who had only thrown five passes in his pro career? The Falcons certainly did not complain, as they were glad to unload Brett, whom they saw as a disappointment. But Ron Wolf knew otherwise.

The other person instrumental in the deal that brought Brett to Green Bay was first-year head coach Mike Holmgren. Long an offensive coordinator for the mighty San Francisco 49ers, Holmgren saw Brett in a preseason scouting camp, before the 1991 draft. He made careful notes on the young quarterback. "Physically he had talent," Holmgren recalled in a 1995 interview, "[He had] a raw ability to throw the ball. He threw every pass the same way: hard, whether it's a five-yarder or a 40-yarder."

Brett was relieved when he heard the news. He said, "I'm surprised it took them that long to trade me. I was there for one year. I didn't play and I can see why they traded me. I was expendable. The Packers gave up a first-round pick for a guy who didn't even play."

The distance from Green Bay, Wisconsin, to Kiln, Mississippi, is about 1,000 miles. However, in some ways it is worlds away. One of the major adjustments Brett had to make early on was to the weather. Northern Wisconsin is known for its cold winters and even in the summer, Green Bay is not what a southerner would call warm. In an interview, Brett recalled the difference between training camp back home and in Green Bay.

Favre wasted no time in showing what he could do once he was traded to the Green Bay Packers. Here he runs for a first down as two Steeler linebackers try to chase him down from behind.

"You know how in training camp in Suwanee, you try to get away with wearing as little as possible? Well, honest to God, here in camp one day—this was July or August—I had three sweat suits on underneath my uniform. It's different, really different." And at this point, Brett had never played at Lambeau Field on a face-and-finger-freezing, mind-numbingly cold December afternoon.

Brett made it through Coach Holmgren's training camp and settled into the backup spot behind Don Majkowski. Majkowski, nicknamed, "The Magic Man," was a rising star with the Pack, and many felt he was going to be the quarterback of the future. However, Majkowski never really got off the ground that season.

In the third week of the 1992 campaign, in a game against the Cincinnati Bengals, Majkowski suffered an ankle injury in the first quarter and was forced to exit the game. Newspaper accounts said he would miss "up to a month" in playing time, but the truth was that he would never play for the Green Bay Packers again. Thrown into the action having thrown more interceptions than completions in his professional career, Brett Favre stepped in and led his team in an unforgettable NFL debut.

With the Packers down 17-3 after three quarters, Favre led a dramatic comeback at Lambeau Field. He was helped by a 58-yard punt return by rookie Terrell Buckley. On the next series, he led the Packers on a drive down to the Bengal 5 yard line, and there he connected with Sterling Sharpe to close the score to 20-17. On their next possession, the Bengals kicked a field goal to open their lead to six points, forcing the Packers to score a touchdown and an extra point if they wanted to win the game.

What happened next will live in Packer memory for years to come. The Pack were pinned back deep in their own territory with 1:07 on the clock and no time-outs. Five plays later, Favre threw a 35-yard pass to Kitrick Taylor with 13 seconds left on the clock for the winning touchdown. The Packers had stolen a victory from a team that thought they had the game won. Brett would repeat this performance many times over in the course of the years that followed.

However, the first few outings after the Cincinnati game proved educational for Brett. The Packers lost four of their next five games, including a 24-10 drubbing by the Atlanta Falcons. It was a game in which Brett played well—he completed 33 of 44 passes for 276 yards—but he could only connect on 1 touchdown pass. Any statement he wanted to make to his former team would have to wait.

The Packers were 3-5 as they entered the second half of the season. The last eight games would see Green Bay playing its toughest teams, including NFC Central rivals: the Minnesota Vikings, Detroit Lions (twice), and Chicago Bears. The playoffs seemed like too much to hope for, but at least the Pack could salvage some pride.

Against Detroit Favre threw for 212 yards and 2 touchdowns as the Packers won, 27-13. This began a remarkable stretch for the Packers in which they were on their way to only their second winning season in 10 years.

As Green Bay entered its final game of the season against the Minnesota Vikings, they were riding the crest of a six-game winning streak. Favre had led the team to thrilling fourth quarter victories over Philadelphia, Tampa Bay, and Houston. They had also handily knocked off the Los Angeles Rams, the Lions, and the Bears. However, even though they were 9-6, they were still not guaranteed a playoff spot. They would have to defeat the Vikings to get it.

Alas, the Vikings were ready for Favre and Green Bay, winning 27-7. The Packers, who had not made the playoffs since 1982, would watch them again on television.

But in Packerland there was still much to be excited about. Brett Favre showed himself to be one of the most promising young quarterbacks in the league. Sterling Sharpe, their great wide receiver, broke Art Monk's single-season reception record. Mike Holmgren, their new coach,

Coach Mike Holmgren confers with the referees about a call.

proved that he was indeed ready to make the jump from successful assistant to successful head coach.

For Favre, even though he was disappointed that the Packers did not make the playoffs, he was delighted to be chosen for the Pro Bowl. The third quarterback picked for the NFC squad, Favre earned his way there by throwing for 3,227 yards and 18 touchdown passes. He joined fellow Packers Sharpe and safety Chuck Cecil on the team.

In talking to reporters the week leading up to the game, Favre brought his wide-eyed enthusiasm and down-home humor to an event that most of the veterans look at as just a nice opportunity to go to Hawaii. When some of the established NFL players, such as Steve Young or Dan Marino, would say hello to him, Favre told reporters, "I'm thinking 'how do they know who I am?' But then again, I was voted in, so somebody must know."

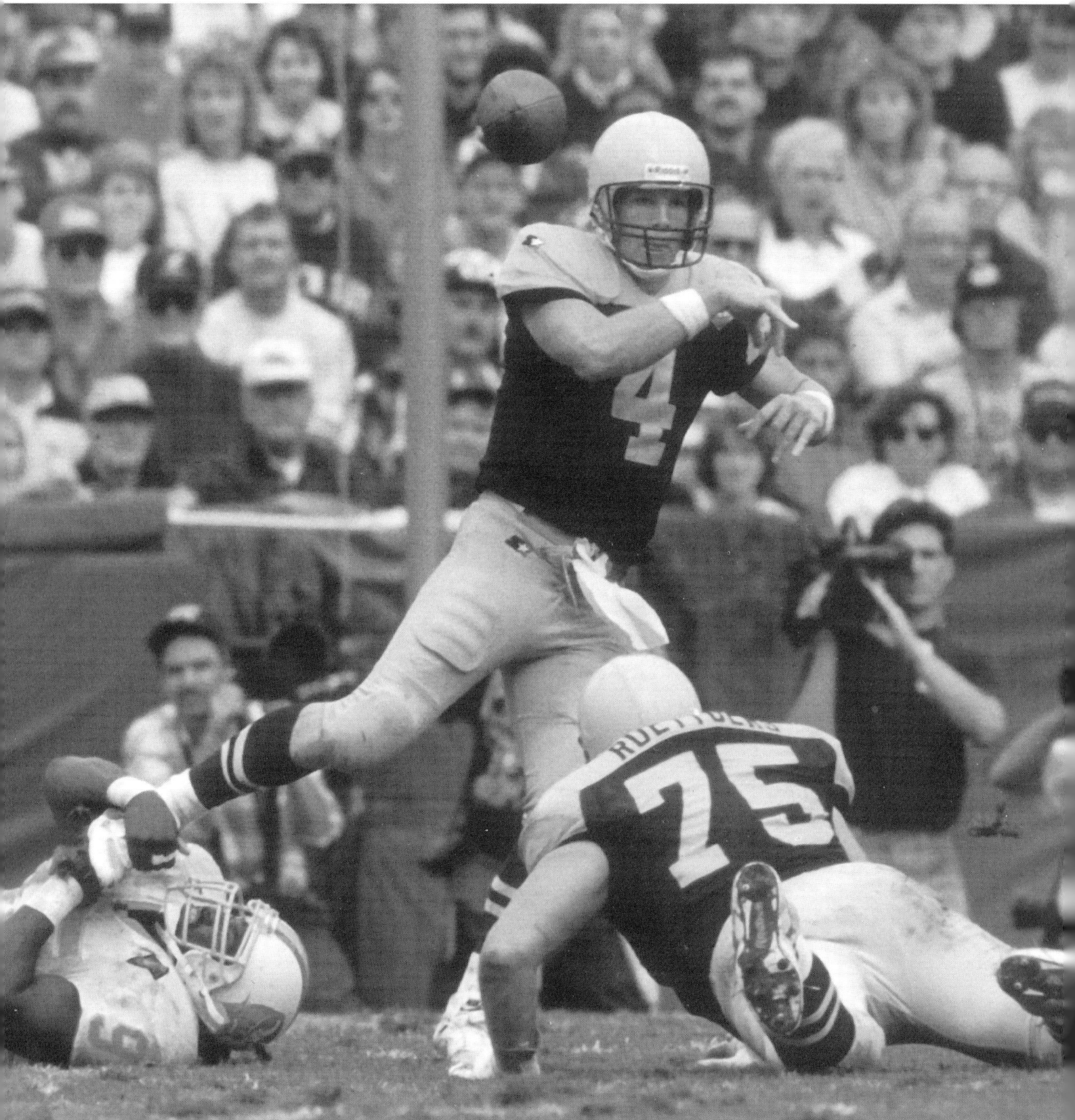

4
"COUNTRY" RIDING HIGH

After his first season with the Packers, Favre began to attract a lot of attention. In short, he became a celebrity. True, his passing ability and leadership skills had led Green Bay to only their second winning season since the strike-shortened season of 1982 and made him a favorite of Packer fans right away. But the other reason had less to do with his football skills than with his personality. The newspapers and television loved his good humor, southern drawl, and brash attitude. He was the first quarterback since Joe Namath and Terry Bradshaw in the 1960s and 1970s and Jim McMahon in the 1980s to combine such tremendous athletic skills with a dynamic personality.

Because of his down-home personality and

In one of his finest outings, Favre completed 30 of 39 passes for 306 yards and three touchdowns against Tampa Bay in 1994. On this play, Favre fires another completion despite having a Buccaneer clutching at his ankle. (In this game, the Packers were wearing old-style uniforms.)

Southern roots, Favre picked up the nickname "Country," and just about every magazine and newspaper article made reference to his upbringing in Kiln. In the fall of 1993, *The New York Times* called him "Li'l Abner with the ability to go deep," a reference to the famous hillbilly cartoon character. One of the images many people would carry of Favre is that of him and his brothers drinking beer and eating crawdads when he got the phone call that he was being traded to Green Bay. Favre said, "Me and my brothers were just having a typical dinner at home. It's like 'I'm traded. Great.' But I didn't want to give up my five pounds of crawfish, you know?"

Favre's reputation as a fun-loving, country bumpkin with the boyish looks and rifle arm was one that endeared him to many. Yet it was also a problem for him because when he did not do well on the field, people criticized his work ethic and dedication to the team.

At the start of the 1993 season, expectations were high. Favre had lifted a team that was 4-12 in 1991 to a 9-7 mark, one game shy of making the playoffs. The talent around him was excellent. Not only was Pro Bowler Sterling Sharpe back, but the Packers also acquired Mark Clayton in the off season. Clayton had long been a deep threat with Dan Marino while playing for the Miami Dolphins. Now Favre would have two dangerous receivers on the field. Clayton cited Favre as one of the main reasons he came to Green Bay, "He showed the league a little last year of what he's capable of doing. He's going to be good. Heck, he's already good. He's going to be great."

The biggest off-season acquisition in the league was the Packer signing of free agent Reggie White in one of the most anticipated moves in NFL history. White had previously been with the Philadelphia Eagles, where he established himself as the premiere pass-rusher in the league. Virtually all big-market and playoff-hopeful teams had courted him but his much-publicized free agency tour culminated with his signing with the Green Bay Packers. He too said that the talent of Brett Favre was one of the main reasons he decided join the Packers.

With all of these pieces in place, it would seem that a playoff berth or a division title were in the bag for the Packers, but after the first four games, Green Bay found itself with a 1-3 record. They were at the bottom of the NFC Central. However, as he had done before, Favre was able to lead

Reggie White, perhaps the greatest defensive lineman ever, chose to play with Green Bay in hopes of winning a Super Bowl. Here Jeff Hostetler, quarterback of the Los Angeles Raiders, is about to be sacked by White.

his team out of the depths of despair. The Packers went on to win six of their next seven games, to take the lead in the Central division, tied with Detroit.

In the last five games, even though the Packers lost to division rivals Chicago, Minnesota, and Detroit, they did secure their first playoff birth in 11 years with victories over San Diego and the Raiders. Despite this success, Favre knew that teams were now ready for him. They knew what he was capable of doing and they keyed their defenses in order to stop him. The young quarterback was frustrated at times, and his numbers showed it. His interceptions were up, and his quarterback rating was down, along with his completion percentage. Although he passed for more total yards in 1993 (3,303), he also played in three more games. Favre's first full season with the Packers was a roller-coaster, but it was one in which the team saw more ups than downs.

The game against the Raiders, as the Packers fought to make the playoffs, was held on the second coldest day in the history of Lambeau Field. (The coldest was the "Ice Bowl" game against the Cowboys in 1967.) Favre threw two touchdown passes to Sterling Sharpe on the icy field, which Favre said, "was like playing on concrete." At kickoff, the temperature was 0 degrees with a wind-chill factor of 22 degrees below. Favre told reporters after the game, "It was so cold that I put Vaseline in places I never thought of before."

The big story, however, was the Packer defense, which completely shut down the Raiders, sacking quarterback Jeff Hostetler eight times. Reggie White accounted for two of the sacks, and he also recovered a fumble, which he lateraled to

LeRoy Butler who returned it for a touchdown.

Cold or no cold, the Packers were in the playoffs. The only thing marring the remainder of the season was a 30-20 loss against the Lions at Detroit. It was an ugly game in which Favre threw four interceptions. In a rare occurrence, he had the chance to redeem himself the very next week, as the NFC wild-card playoff game pitted the Packers against none other than the Lions.

In one of the wildest playoff games in recent memory, a see-saw battle in which the lead changed hands five times, the Green Bay Packers made their first playoff appearance in 11 years an unforgettable one. The game featured 703 yards in total offense. There were two interception returns for touchdowns, one by the Lions, and one by the Packers—a 101-yard run by safety George Teague, which gave the Packers a 21-17 lead going into the fourth quarter.

This was a day in which neither defense could stop the other team's offense. Barry Sanders, the great Lions halfback, rushed for 169 yards, including one run of 44 yards. Lion receiver Brett Perriman caught 10 passes for 150 yards. Things looked dark for the Packers as Detroit jumped ahead halfway into the fourth quarter on a five-yard touchdown run by Derrick Moore. The score stayed 24-21 Lions until Favre and the Packers took over with less than a minute to go in the game.

Time was running out in the Pontiac Silverdome as Favre scrambled to his left, looking desperately for an open receiver. So many times he had sparked the Packers to come-from-behind victories. Would there be another trick in Favre's magic bag? The answer lay in the hands of Ster-

Favre threw four touchdown passes to Sterling Sharpe in a 1994 regular-season game against the Cowboys. Nevertheless, Dallas won, 42-31.

ling Sharpe, who found himself open some 60 yards downfield behind the last defender in what was supposed to be a prevent defense. Sharpe pulled in the ball and landed safely in the Detroit end zone, shocking the hometown crowd of more than 68,000 people.

After the game, Favre told reporters, "It was not planned. It was like drawing it up in the sand." He was so excited after the win that he told *Sports Illustrated*, "I lost my helmet, my ear pads. I started hyperventilating. I was looking for someone to kiss."

The elation of that week was short-lived however, as the Packers faced the defending Super Bowl champion Dallas Cowboys in the divisional playoff game in Texas. Although the Cowboys turned the ball over three times in the first half, the Packers could not capitalize and they lost the game 27-17. Dallas just had too much for the Pack that day. While Favre was able to pass for more than 300 yards and 2 touchdowns, the Packers never really could get close to the Cowboys.

Favre had accomplished many of the things he and the team set out to do in 1993, yet he had much to work on and think about in the off-season. While the Packers did make the playoffs, and did have back-to-back winning seasons for the first time since the Lombardi era, Favre's performance was erratic. The most telling statistic was the number of interceptions he threw, 24, to the number of touchdown passes, 19. Numbers like that do not keep you in a starting quarterback position for long. Favre knew that if he was going to take his team to the next level, he was going to have to make fewer mistakes.

The roller coaster ride continued for the Packers in the 1994 season, but Favre's performance became much more consistent. After signing a five-year, $19-million contract, all eyes were on the 25-year-old phenom.

Green Bay had another up-and-down season. As usual, nothing came easily for Favre. The Pack was 6-7 with three games left and would have to win them all in order to have a chance at making the playoffs.

The next game brought the Atlanta Falcons, who were also fighting for a playoff spot. And with less than two minutes left, it looked like they were going to satisfy that goal. However, in the NFL, two minutes can be a lifetime, and with Favre at the helm, it was all the time the Packers would need. Starting from his own 33 yard line, Favre led the Packers on a march to the Atlanta 9 with 21 seconds left and no time-outs. With only enough time for two more plays from scrimmage, Favre set up in the pocket; all of his receivers were covered. Instead of taking the safe way out and throwing the ball out of the end zone, Favre ran. With Jumpy Geathers and Chuck Smith in hot pursuit, Favre dug down deep and was able to outrace the two defenders to the end zone. "I never thought I'd run it in," he later told reporters, "The end zone looked farther and farther away as I got closer to it."

The win against Atlanta helped propel the Pack past Tampa Bay the next week, thus guaranteeing a playoff berth for the second year in a row. With a victory in their last game, the Pack finished with a 9-7 record.

The 1994 season represented a real maturation for Favre. He became a much more consistent quarterback, able to read the complex NFL defenses with more confidence and able to make better decisions on the field. He cut his interceptions to 14, 10 fewer than the year before, and his total passing yardage rose to 3882. In addition, he broke Lynn Dickey's touchdown passing record with 33 and also broke Don Majkowski's single season completion record, with 363, 10 more than the Magic Man. Finally, Favre's quarterback rating number was up to 90.7, 28 points higher than the season before. (The quarterback rating is a formula derived from a quarterback's completion rate, interceptions, and other vital statistics.)

In a carbon copy of the year before, the Pack beat the Detroit Lions in another closely contested battle, 16-12. The Packers defense was amazing, holding Barry Sanders to negative one yard on the ground. Even though Sanders was stopped, the Lions had a chance to win the game in the closing seconds, but on their final possession of the game, the Lions were stopped on the 17 yard line when Packer safety George Teague knocked receiver Herman Moore out of the end zone after he caught a Dave Krieg fourth down pass. Favre passed for 262 yards in the victory.

Again, repeating the previous year's history, the Packers traveled to Texas to face the Cowboys, and for the second time in two years they were beaten soundly by Aikman, Smith, Irvin, and Co. The Cheeseheads (a fond nickname for Packer fans) were sent back to Wisconsin aching from a 35-9 thrashing by the two-time defending world champions.

After the game, in which he was 18 for 36 for 216 yards, Favre was philosophical. "Hell, there were 22 teams sitting at home watching us play," he said. But he gave credit where it was due. "I have to tip my hat to Dallas, but there are a lot of positives to take from this game." It was upon those positives that Favre would build, and he would be ready, in 1995, to have the season of his life.

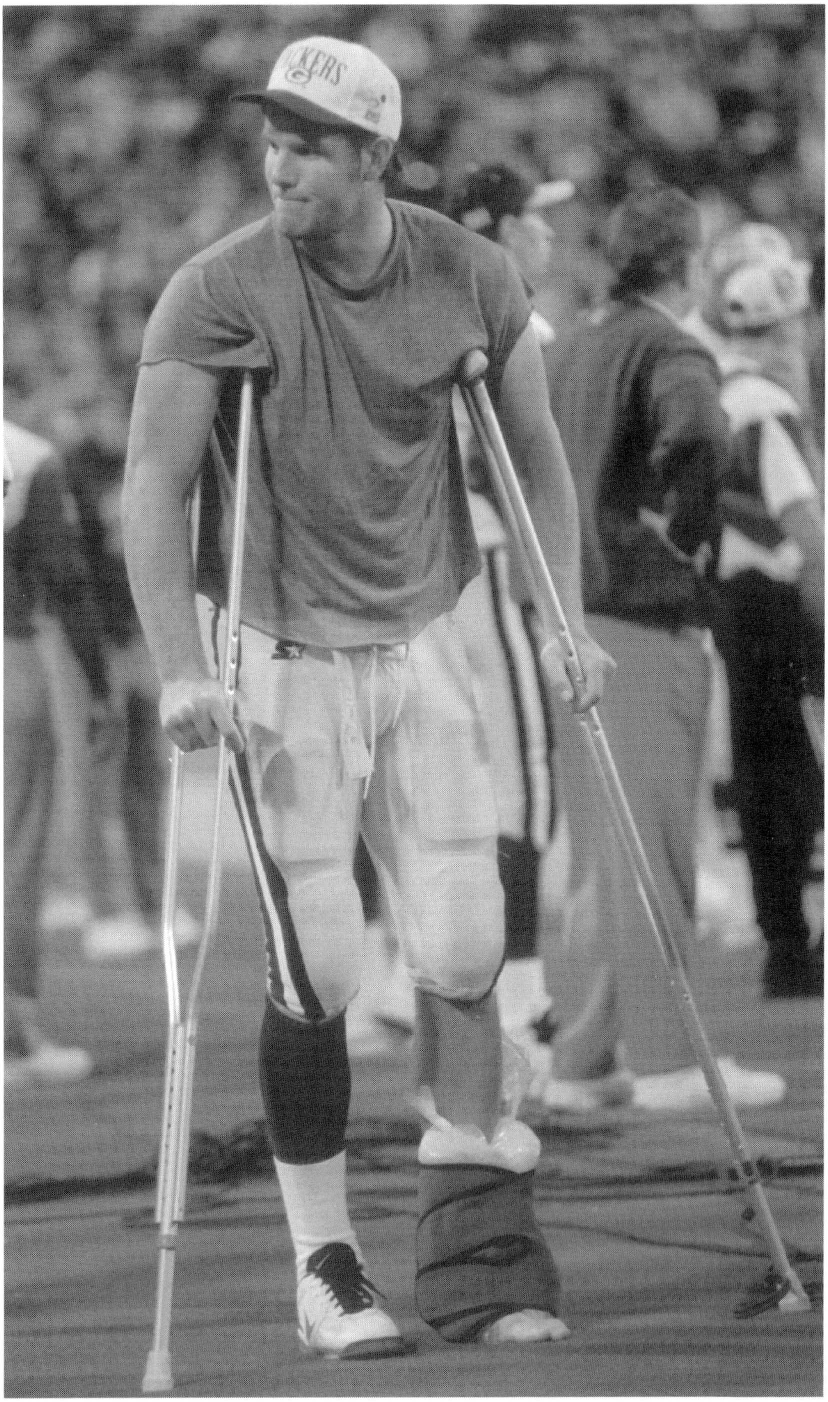

5
PUTTING IT ALL TOGETHER

When the 1995 season started, Brett Favre was one of the National Football League's new superstars. In 1994, he proved to those who doubted his ability and commitment that he was ready to take the next step. If Green Bay was going to compete with the Dallas Cowboys for the NFC championship, he and the rest of the Packers were going to have to play the best football of their lives. With all of the doubts about Favre's talents and maturity as a quarterback gone, however, he became the number one target of opposing teams on game day in the violent world of professional football.

In the NFL, the highest praise a player can receive is that he is a "gamer," someone who, week in and week out, plays his heart out and gets his job done, no matter what. There is no doubt that football on any level is a rough sport. When you consider the speed, size, strength,

An injury during the 1995 game against the Vikings forced Favre to watch the rest of the game in frustration.

and will-to-win of the NFL player, you can understand that, given the nature of the game, players are going to get injured. The challenge of all professional players is to stay in shape and avoid injury as best as possible. In Favre's years as a college and pro, however, he has suffered a variety of injuries, but he is a gamer. Since coming off the bench against the Bengals in 1992, Favre has never missed a start at quarterback. At the start of the 1996 season, his string of 68 consecutive regular and post-season starts is the longest of all current NFL quarterbacks.

In the last six years, Favre has had surgery on his back, his intestines, his shoulder (suffered in 1992 on a vicious hit from then-Philadelphia Eagle Reggie White), and on muscles on his right side below his ribs. None of these injuries have ever kept him from starting a game. But they have taken their toll. Favre was 26 years old during the 1995 season when his wife, Deanna, told *Sports Illustrated* that when he gets out of bed on Monday mornings, "he looks like such an old man."

Deanna and Brett have known each other for a long time; they started dating in the ninth grade. At the start of his career, Favre spent much of his time traveling back and forth between Green Bay and Kiln, where Deanna lived with their daughter, Britanny. Up until 1995, Favre and Deanna still did not have a permanent home in Wisconsin. Even though the family is often apart, they are very close.

When the team is on the road, Favre will often call home to say goodnight to his daughter. One night before a game Favre asked her how many touchdown passes she wanted him to throw the next day, and she said, "Three." He went out

PUTTING IT
ALL TOGETHER

against the Buffalo Bills and threw three. The following week, he called again, and Britanny said she wanted to see four touchdowns—against the Dallas Cowboys. Favre gulped and said, "That's hard against Dallas." But he went out and did it. Before the game against the Chicago Bears, she asked him, "Do you think you could throw five?" He only managed to throw three, though two were just short; one was dropped in the end zone, and one receiver was tackled at the 1 yard line. "Doggone it," Favre said, "if there wasn't a point in the game where I thought I could." As banged up as Favre's body is, his heart is always in the right place.

Favre's heart is one of the things that has earned him a reputation in the Green Bay area. Some football players get caught up in their own fame, and they sometimes forget about the "little" people in their lives. But Favre has not forgotten. He is very active in Green Bay and NFL charities, he hosts a celebrity golf tournament for charity in Mississippi, and he has a great deal of respect for all of the people around him.

Green Bay's 1995 season got off to a typically disappointing start when they lost 17-14 to the surprising St. Louis Rams. Nevertheless, Favre and the Packers showed what they were made of and won five of their next six games. Their only fall was a 34-24 loss to the Cowboys, who, under new coach Barry Switzer, were out to recapture the Super Bowl after losing it to the San Francisco 49ers the year before.

Some experts predicted the Packers would suffer greatly from the loss of Sterling Sharpe, who was forced to retire in December 1994 because of a serious spinal injury. Sharpe had been Favre's most dangerous receiver and just the year before he had set a record for most passes caught.

The Packers figured out a way to make up for the loss of Sharpe. Although no other pass catcher on the team could singly fill his shoes, Favre started to use his other receivers more extensively. In the past, Sharpe had been Favre's main target, and the defenses knew it—even if they still couldn't always prevent it. In 1995, for the first time in his career, Favre started to spread the ball out to many different players. Consider the Detroit game in October. In the Packers' 30-21 defeat of the Lions, Favre threw the ball to six different receivers, including four to wideout Robert Brooks, four to running back Edgar Bennett, four to wide receiver Mark Ingram, and four to fullback Dorsey Levans. Clearly, opposing defenses would have to concentrate their efforts all over the field now, and Favre took full advantage of their problem.

An example of this new-found strength came in a game against the Chicago Bears at Soldier Field. On a third and 10 from his own 1 yard line, Favre was under heavy pressure from a Chicago blitz. He saw Brooks turn around defensive back Donnel Woolford and somehow got the ball to him. Ninety-nine yards later, Brooks was in the end zone, and the Packers had just completed the longest pass play in Soldier Field history, and only the eighth 99-yard TD pass in NFL history.

As the season progressed, Favre performed brilliantly and often valiantly. In the week 10 game against the Vikings, however, he did not have such a great day. In that game, he was 17 for 30 with only 177 yards passing, 0 touchdowns, and 2 interceptions. To top it off, he severely injured his left ankle at the end of the third quarter and backup Ty Detmer was called in to take over. This left the Packers with a 5-4 record and a two consecutive losses. Many people were indeed wondering if this was a different team at all.

Even though his left ankle had not completely healed—as a matter of fact it was still very swollen and discolored at game time, and Favre walked with a considerable limp—Brett started against the Bears the next week. In one of his most heroic performances, he lifted the Packers to a 35-28 victory over Chicago. He threw for 336 yards, completing over 70 percent of his passes, five for touchdowns, and no interceptions. Britanny finally had her five-TD game, and the Packers went on to win five of their next six games en route to an NFC Central division championship.

The year ended up being an extremely good one for Favre. He posted the best numbers of his career and shook the reputation of being inconsistent and streaky. On the season he threw for 4,413 yards with 38 touchdown passes, breaking his previous club record. His interceptions were down to 13, with only two in the last seven games. His quarterback rating of 99.5 was the best in the league.

All of these accomplishments were good, but Favre wanted to lead his team to a championship,

Robert Brooks leaps into the stands among adoring fans after catching his second touchdown pass from Brett Favre in a 1995 game against Chicago. Mark Chmura also helps Brooks celebrate the score.

to another shot at the Dallas Cowboys. To do that the Packers would have to clear a couple of hurdles in the playoffs first.

The first of those hurdles came against the Atlanta Falcons, and the Packers cleared it with ease. Favre threw three touchdown passes against the team that had traded him four years before, and the Pack prevailed 37-20 in front of the hometown fans at Lambeau Field. The win kept the Packers undefeated in playoff games at the historic site. The game featured a new ritual for the Packers: after scoring a touchdown, the Packer who had scored would jump into the stands. In a statement revealing the great love the Packers have for residents of Green Bay, and vice-versa, Robert Brooks said, "we want to entertain the fans who pay our salaries."

Packer fans were even more entertained with the result of the next week's game against the San Francisco 49ers. In a game San Francisco tackle Steve Wallace called an "old-fashioned butt-kicking," the Packers dominated the defending Super Bowl champions on the ground and in the air on offense. Reggie White, though suffering from a hamstring injury, led the defense in shutting down Steve Young, Jerry Rice, and company. Not since the days of Lombardi, Starr, and Ray Nitschke 30 years before had there been this much excitement in Green Bay. For Favre, after his 21-for-28, 299-yard, two-touchdown performance, he was uncharacteristically low-keyed. When asked about his game, he responded only, "I'm not going to lie to you, I'm happy with how I played." He had something else on his mind. That something else was the Dallas Cowboys, who beat the Philadelphia Eagles the next day in Irving, Texas.

The Cowboys had defeated the Green Bay Packers in their last six meetings, dating back to 1991. Those losses included the last two years in the playoffs. As a developing team, the Packers were overmatched by the Cowboys, who had already established themselves as one of the most dominant teams in professional football. Owner Jimmy Jones had stockpiled his team with an unusual number of All-Pro players, figuring out the loopholes in the salary cap rules like no one else. Although Dallas had lost to the 49ers the year before, that only made them more determined to win in the 1996 NFC Championship Game. Peter King of *Sports Illustrated* wrote, "The Green Bay Packers desperately wanted to win this NFC title game. The Cowboys had to win."

Although Favre and the Packers put in their gutsiest performance to date against the Cowboys, they made too many errors at crucial moments and when the Cowboys really needed that something extra, they always found it. Favre started out the day very poorly—his first six passes were incomplete—but he was able to put it together in the first half tossing two touchdown passes, one to Keith Jackson, and a 76-yarder to Robert Brooks, to keep the Packers in the game. At the end of the first half, the Packers trailed 24-17.

In the third quarter, a Chris Jacke field goal brought the Pack to within four points. On their next possession, Favre led the offensive on another impressive drive, which culminated with a one-yard pass from Favre to Robert Brooks. The Packers finally had the lead, 27-24.

A three-point lead, however, is not a very big cushion against a team as powerful as the Cow-

Gilbert Brown (93), John Jurkovic (64), Matt LaBounty (97), and LeRoy Butler (36) gang tackle Craig Heyward in Green Bay's victory over Atlanta in the 1995 NFC wild card playoff game. Asked why the Packers won, Butler responded, "Brett, Brett, and Brett."

boys. In the opening minutes of the fourth quarter, Dallas quarterback Troy Aikman put together a 14-play drive that featured a mix of run and pass plays, ending with Emmitt Smith's five-yard touchdown run. The 90-yard march made the score 31-27, but there were still 12 minutes left and Packers were in the ball game. For the first time in three years, Green Bay was toe-to-toe with the Cowboys, the team that had dismissed them handily in their last two encounters.

On the next series, Favre drove the Pack into Dallas territory, but then threw a pass to receiver Mark Ingram that was picked off by cornerback Larry Brown. A couple of plays later, a pass of 36 yards to Michael Irvin extended the Cowboys' lead, then a 16-yard TD run by Emmitt Smith, his third of the day, made the score 38-27 and sewed up the game.

On the day, Favre was 21 for 39 for 307 yards. His two touchdown passes, however, were overshadowed by the two interceptions he threw.

Nevertheless, this was an important game for the Packers. In beating the 49ers they had proved they were for real, and in playing so tough against the Cowboys, they proved they had arrived as one of the elite teams in the league. While the loss was a tough one to take, after the game Favre reflected on what the game meant: "It's been a stepladder the last couple of seasons. I'd like to think that next year will be the Super Bowl. This year was a great run. We had some great wins, some tough losses. This is one of the tough losses."

Favre went on, "We didn't panic. We came back and that's where we are different than in the past."

A few days before the playoff win against San Francisco, Brett Favre was named the Most Valuable Player in the National Football League for the 1995 season. Based upon his throwing for more than 4,400 yards and 38 touchdown passes, his quarterback rating of 99.5, and his low interception rate, including a string of 113 passes without a pick, Favre easily beat out the great San Francisco wide receiver Jerry Rice for the honor. At the press conference announcing the award, it was vintage Favre. Unshaven and wearing a hooded sweatshirt to answer questions from the press, Favre showed that success had not gone to the head of the country boy from Mississippi.

A week after the Dallas Cowboys knocked off the Pittsburgh Steelers for their fifth Super Bowl championship, Favre was named the starting quarterback for the NFC in the Pro Bowl. Twenty-six years old and a long way from his last appearance there in 1993, he was honored to be named the starter, but was still aching to play in the Super Bowl. "It's been a great year for me and my teammates," he told reporters, "I'd much rather culminate my year with a trip to the Super Bowl, but this is still a great way to end things because you're voted here by your peers."

What Favre did not say at the Pro Bowl was that he was aching physically, too. The season was a successful one in many ways, but his body took a tremendous pounding. His desire to win, to play with pain, and to ignore the messages his body was sending him would catch up with Favre. The truth of the matter was that Favre was taking prescription painkillers to help him make it through the season.

Favre's dependence on the drug Vicodin became frighteningly clear to him in a Green Bay hospital in February 27, 1996, when he lapsed into a seizure following an operation to remove bone chips from his ankle. The seizure, which occurred in the presence of his wife and daughter, was a message from his body that he could no longer ignore. His wife Deanna told *Sports Illustrated* that at least one time he had taken as many as 13 of the pills in a single day.

Following the scary episode, Favre entered treatment programs monitored by drug counselors from the NFL. Favre was not suspended by the league because he volunteered news of his drug dependency and took positive steps to deal with it. Nevertheless, the league will continue to watch Favre closely, and if he is found to be using any drugs, including alcohol, he could be subject to league discipline. Such disciplinary measures start with a four-game suspension and get tougher with further lapses.

Known for his brash Southern humor and outgoing personality, it was a somber Brett Favre who appeared at a May 14 press conference to announce his dependence on prescription drugs. "Throughout the last couple of years, playing with pain and injuries and because of numerous surgeries, I became dependent upon medication," he told a throng of reporters gathered in Green Bay. He cited his February seizure as the event that brought his problem into focus for him. "Because of that," he said "I sought help through the NFL. I think the best thing to do was get some help. That's what we're going to do."

The next day, Favre entered a treatment facility in Kansas where he took part in a drug and alcohol dependency program. Support for Favre came from his teammates, but also from players around the league, who understood that Favre is not alone in his addiction. He is one of many NFL players caught in a very difficult situation. Faced with the pressure of performing well for the team, the coaches, and the fans and doing what is best for your body, many players do what they have to do to get in the game. If taking prescription painkillers means they can play, they will do it. It has also been the history of the NFL and the individual teams to turn a blind eye to such abuses. Players like Favre put fans in the seats and numbers on the scoreboard; teams cannot afford to have them injured.

When these pressures are put onto players with the competitive drive of an NFL star, the temptation to turn to drugs that will help them ignore the pain and play is almost unbearable. Favre recalled the time, in his seventh start for the Packers, when he separated his shoulder against the Eagles. He told *Sports Illustrated* that he saw the man he replaced, Don Majkowski, "rarin' to go" on the sidelines, and decided he would have doctors inject his injured shoulder with Novocain to numb the pain so he could continue. "In a little while I didn't feel any pain. I played well, and we won the game. I thought, damn, that was easy." After that, season-by-season, the more hits he took, the more his body ached, and the more he took to taking pain killers. Finally, his body said, "Enough."

Nine weeks after entering the treatment program he was released. In early July 1996, a few weeks before training camp, he faced reporters again and seemed ready to take on the challenge of not only leading his team to victory, but keeping himself drug and alcohol free.

Standing up there in front of all the cameras was the NFL's Most Valuable Player, about to face the toughest challenge of his life. He came back more upbeat than he had been in May, but he was also determined as well. On the field he had come to symbolize resiliency and toughness under pressure. Now, he had come to symbolize the real problem of drugs in the National Football League. Instead of the mythic, invincible heroes the fans think professional football players to be, Favre showed that indeed, they were human, with the same human failings we all have. Favre's admission of his problem and his willingness to address the issue showed him to be as brave as he had ever been on the football field. The challenge that lay ahead of him was a daunting one, but in early July he seemed resolved to overcome it.

"The bottom line is I just don't want this to ever happen again," he said. "Believe me when I tell you that this is going to be hard, but I have faced tougher trials and succeeded. I will not allow myself to be defeated by this challenge." On that day in early July, it was clear that Favre would triumph over this, yet another challenge in his life. After all, he has made a career of beating the odds.

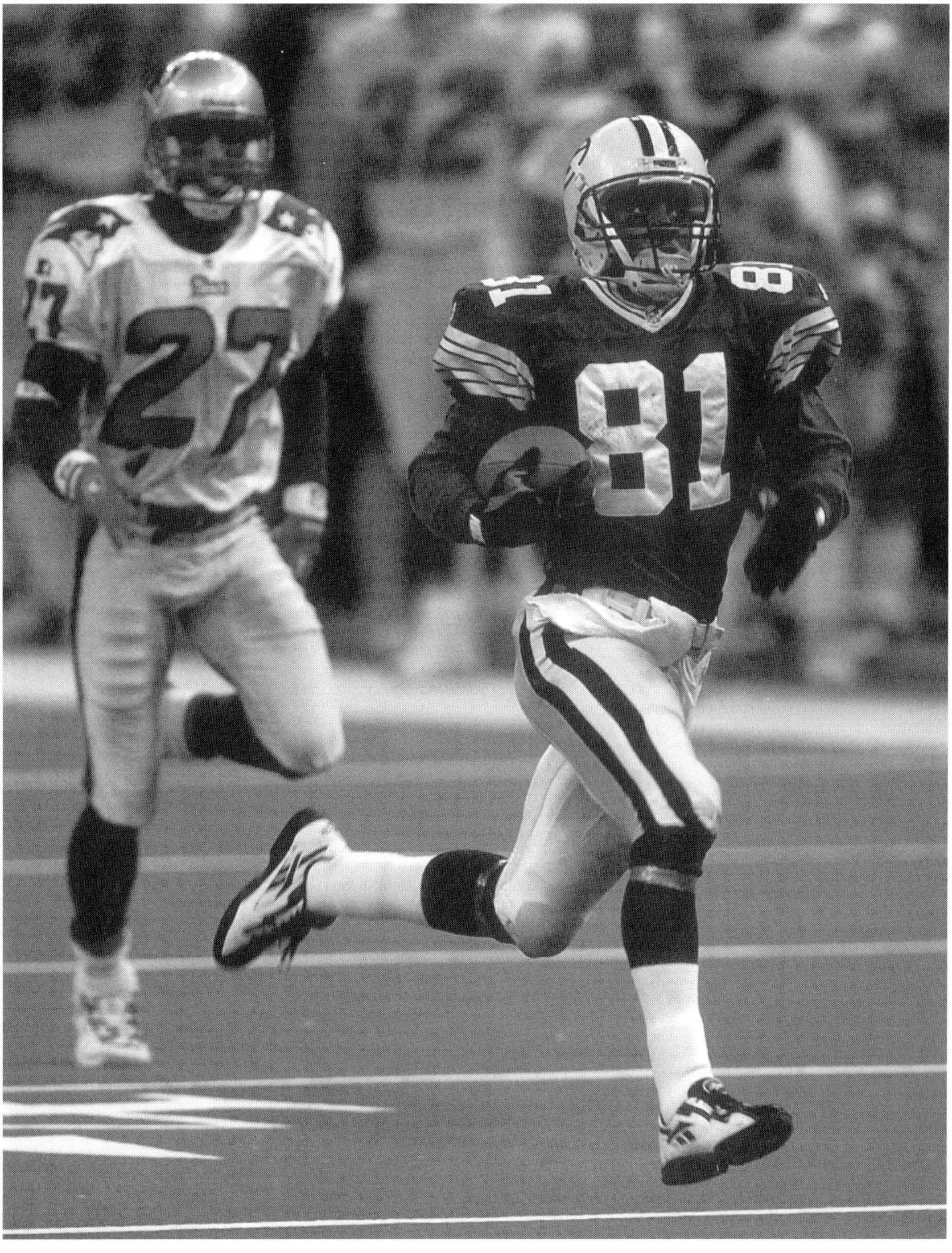
27
81

6
THE ROAD TO NEW ORLEANS

When a reporter asked Favre if after his drug rehab he would be able to reach the same level as his MVP 1995 season, Brett just winked and said, "Don't bet against me."

If there were any doubts about whether or not Brett was back, they were quickly put aside after the first three games of the season. In dispatching Tampa Bay, Philadelphia, and San Diego, the Packers outscored their opponents 115-26. Brett threw for 10 touchdowns in the first three games, and 19 in his first six games. By Week 10, the Pack was 8-1, the best start the franchise had ever had.

This early success did not come without a price, however. Green Bay's best receiver—and Brett's favorite target—Michael Brooks, went down with a season-ending shoulder injury. Brooks's injury, combined with the loss of Antonio Freeman, left a void in the receiving corps

Desmond Howard (81) cruises for a 99-yard kickoff return against the Patriots in Super Bowl XXXI. Howard was named the MVP of the Super Bowl.

Ron Wolf (right) shares laughs with the two quarterbacks he helped bring to Green Bay, Jim McMahon (left) and Brett Favre.

that was filled ably by Don Beebe, Don Mickens, and mid-season replacement Andre Rison.

Back-to-back losses to Kansas City and Dallas were not as stinging, however, as they might have been. In fact, the Cheeseheads then went on another tear, winning the last five games over St. Louis, Chicago, Denver, Detroit, and gaining revenge against Minnesota, the only team to beat them in the first half of the season. After being severely beaten by the Packers, 41-6, the Denver Broncos, who had been considered the best team in the AFC, were never the same.

The Pack finished the season with a 13-3 record and home field advantage in the playoffs. (And what an advantage—the Packers have never lost a playoff game at Lambeau Field, ever!) They had the number-two-ranked offense in the NFC, fifth in the league. Their defense was the stingiest in the league and ranked number one overall.

Over the course of this tremendous run, Brett built up the finest numbers of his career as well. He finished the season with 325 completions out of 543 attempts for a league leading 3,899 yards, with only 13 interceptions, a very low number for so many passing attempts. His most impressive statistic was 39 touchdown passes, one more than his 1995 season, and 17 more than his nearest competitor, Bobby Hebert of the Falcons.

For his outstanding accomplishments in the 1996 season, Brett was awarded his second straight Most Valuable Player Award, beating

John Elway in the voting by a wide margin. With this MVP trophy, Brett joined some exclusive NFL company. Only Joe Montana has also won back-to-back MVP trophies. The great Cleveland running back Jim Brown and Baltimore Colts quarterback Johnny Unitas as well as Steve Young are the only others who have ever won it more than once. Brown and Unitas are already in the Hall of Fame. Montana is a shoo-in once he is eligible, and Young is also a likely candidate for induction.

In winning the award, Brett said, "This year it was like a big weight was lifted off my shoulders. It was like, 'Whew man, this is great.' This is another huge award that made up for a lot of bad things that have happened."

The Packers trounced San Francisco in their first playoff round. But a matchup against the Dallas Cowboys would have to wait at least another year, as the surprising Carolina Panthers upended the defending Super Bowl champions.

In the NFC title game, the Panthers were able to jump out to an early 7-0 lead, but they were no match for the Packer juggernaut. Green Bay broke the game open in the second quarter with touchdown passes from Favre to Dorsey Levens and Antonio Freeman. A Chris Jacke field goal made it 17-10 at the half. In the third quarter, Edgar Bennett capped a 74-yard scoring drive—including a 66-yard Favre-to-Dorsey Levens pass—with a four-yard touchdown run. The Packers never looked back. After the game they were preparing for a date with the New England Patriots in Super Bowl XXXI.

In many ways, this Super Bowl looked to be a mismatch. The Packers had the NFL's best quarterback and best defense. They also had a distinguished history and the near misses in recent years. In addition, the Super Bowl was to be played in New Orleans, just an hour away from Kiln, MS. Most of the fans would be rooting for the hometown hero.

On the other hand, the New England Patriots had, just two years before, been one of the NFL's worst teams. But under the direction of Bill Parcells, who won a couple of Super Bowls with the New York Giants in 1986 and 1991, the Pats had been the surprise team of the year. Drew Bledsoe was considered a strong-armed but inconsistent young quarterback.

Not wasting any time, Brett and company got right to work. On only their second offensive play of the game, Favre hit Andre Rison for a 54-yard scoring strike. After taking advantage of the first of four Drew Bledsoe interceptions with a Chris Jacke field goal, Green Bay took a 10-0 lead in the first quarter, and many were thinking this was going to be another Super Blowout. However, New England came back in the first quarter with two quick scores; Bledsoe connected with Keith Byars and later with Ben Coates. At the end of the first quarter, the score was 14-10 and the Pack was fighting for its life.

But with only a minute gone in the second quarter, Favre saw that Antonio Freeman was getting single coverage by a safety. Brett called an audible and he and Freeman hooked up for a Super Bowl record 81-yard touchdown pass. The score gave the Packers the lead again, and they would not relinquish it.

The exclamation point in the second quarter came when Brett capped a nine-play, 74-yard drive with a two-yard scamper into the end zone.

In one of the game's most exciting plays, Brett ran to the corner, and with his whole body suspended in the air, but out of bounds, he was able to just place the ball over the goal line. At halftime, the Packers led 27-14.

The star of the day was the former Heisman Trophy winner, Desmond Howard. His punt and kickoff returns put Green Bay in excellent field position all day, and his 99-yard kickoff return for a touchdown in the third quarter was the icing on the cake. In what was most likely a

Favre celebrates after throwing a touchdown to Andre Rison in the 1997 Super Bowl. Favre's performance brought a championship back to Green Bay for the first time since 1968.

close race between him and Favre, Desmond Howard was awarded the Super Bowl MVP.

At the end of the third quarter, the score was 35-21 Packers, and that's where it remained. The league's best defense tightened up on the Pats, and with three Reggie White quarterback sacks—another Super Bowl record—the Patriots saw their chances fade. When all was said and done, the Packers were the world champions, and the Patriots were the 13th straight AFC team to be defeated in the Super Bowl.

Reflecting on the victory and the trials and tribulations of the previous year, Brett said "I've been through a lot of tough times this year, and a lot of good. They kind of equal themselves out and you take the good with the bad. To win this, it's unbelievable. It's hard to even talk about it. It definitely makes this past year seem a little better."

Even at the height of his success, Favre was not satisfied. "I've done everything I possibly can," he told reporters after the game. "But I'm very greedy; now I want to win more Super Bowls."

As Brett would say: Don't bet against him.

STATISTICS

BRETT FAVRE

CAREER

Year	Team	G	ATT	CMP	PCT	YDS	INT	TD	RTG
1991	Atl	2	5	0	0	0	0	0	0
1992	GB	15	471	302	64.1	3327	18	13	85.3
1993	GB	16	522	318	60.3	3703	**24**	19	76.2
1994	GB	16	582	363	62.4	3882	14	33	90.7
1995	GB	16	570	359	63.0	**4413**	13	**38**	99.5
1996	GB	16	543	325	59.9	3899	13	**39**	95.8
1997	GB	16	513	304	59.2	3867	16	35	92.6
TOTALS		97	3206	1971	61.5	23091	98	177	90.1

G games
ATT attempts
CMP completions
PCT percent
YDS yards
INT interceptions
TD touchdowns
RTG quarterback rating

bold indicates league-leading statistics

BRETT FAVRE
A CHRONOLOGY

1969   Born on October 10 in Kiln, Mississippi

1986   Enters the University of Southern Mississippi and red-shirts his first year

1987   First year as a starter for the Golden Eagles; sets school record with 14 touchdown passes

1988   Leads USM to victory over UTEP in Independence Bowl; breaks his own single-season record for touchdown passes with 16; sets single-season passing yardage record with 2,271; named to first team All-Metro Conference

1989   Breaks record for passing yards in a season with 2,588; daughter Britanny born

1990   Injured in car accident and misses first game of the season at USM; comes back in second game to lead Eagles to upset win over Alabama

1991   Drafted in the second round by the Atlanta Falcons

1992   Traded to the Green Bay Packers for first round draft pick; comes off the bench for the injured Don Majkowski and leads the Packers to a 9-7 record; named to Pro Bowl

1993   Favre throws for more than 3000 yards as Packers make the playoffs for the first time in 11 years

1994   Throws Packer record 33 touchdown passes en route to second straight playoff appearance

1995   Favre has best season of his career, passing for 4413 yards with 38 touchdowns and only 13 interceptions and is named MVP; Packers win NFC Central division title with 11-5 record

1996   Favre admits to pain killer abuse in May; released from treatment center in July; married long time girlfriend Deanna Tynes in July; named NFL's MVP

1997   Leads Packers to 35-21 Super Bowl victory, over the New England Patriots; inducted into the Southern Mississippi Hall of Fame; Packers win the division title with a 13-3 record

1998   Packers lose Super Bowl to Denver Broncos, 31-24

Suggestions for Further Reading

Diefenbach, Dan, "One on One" *Sport Magazine*, November, 1995.

Fuson, Ken, "Guts or Glory." *Esquire*, October 1996.

King, Peter, "Bitter Pill." *Sports Illustrated*, May 27, 1996.

Murphy, Austin, "Green Machine." *Sports Illustrated*, September 23, 1996.

Telander, Rick, "Pass . . . or Fail " *Sports Illustrated*, January 17, 1994.

About the Author

Marty Mooney is the Assistant Director of College Advising at The Hill School in Pottstown, Pennsylvania, where he is an instructor of English and a football coach as well. A graduate of Dartmouth College, where he played his collegiate football, Marty and his wife, Danielle, have two children, Katherine and Megan, and two dogs. Marty is also the author of *The Comanche Indians*, in Chelsea House's Junior Library of American Indians.

INDEX

Aikman, Troy, 11, 39, 48
Beebe, Don, 56
Bennett, Edgar, 44, 57
Bradshaw, Terry, 31
Brooks, Robert, 8, 9, 44, 45, 47, 55
Brown, Gilbert, 48
Brown, Jim, 56
Brown, Larry, 48
Buckley, Terrell, 27
Butler, LeRoy, 34, 48
Byars, Keith, 58
Cecil, Chuck, 29
Chmura, Mark, 8, 10, 45
Clayton, Mark, 32
Coates, Ben, 58
Dickey, Lynn, 38
Elway, John, 56
Favre, Bonita, 13, 16
Favre, Brandi, 14
Favre, Brett
  honors received, 18, 21, 29, 49, 56-57
  injuries of, 19, 41, 42, 45, 50, 51
Favre, Britanny, 42-43
Favre, Deanna, 42, 50
Favre, Irvin, 13-14, 16
Favre, Jeff, 14
Favre, Scott, 14, 19
Freeman, Antonio, 56, 57, 59
French, Izella, 15

Geathers, Jumpy, 38
Glanville, Jerry, 25
Guy, Ray, 16
Hanks, Merton, 10
Hebert, Bobby, 57
Heyward, Craig, 48
Holmgren, Mike, 8, 24, 25, 27, 29
Hostetler, Jeff, 33, 34
Howard, Desmond, 55, 59
Ingram, Mark, 44, 48
Irvin, Michael, 11, 39, 48
Jacke, Chris, 9, 57, 58
Jackson, Keith, 8, 9, 10, 11, 47
Jones, Jimmy, 47
Jurkovic, John, 8, 48
King, Peter, 47
Krieg, Dave, 39
LaBounty, Matt, 48
Levans, Dorsey, 44, 57
Lipps, Louis, 16
Loescher, Keith, 19
Lombardi, Vinc, 8, 46
Majkowski, Don, 26, 38, 52
Marino, Dan, 15, 29, 32
Marinovich, Todd, 23
McGwire, Dan, 23
McMahon, Jim, 31, 57
Mickens, Don, 56
Miller, Chris, 25
Monk, Art, 29
Montana, Joe, 56

Moore, Derrick, 35
Moore, Herman, 39
Nagle, Browning, 24
Namath, Joe, 31
Newsome, Craig, 9
Nitschke, Ray, 46
Rice, Jerry, 7, 10, 46, 49
Rison, Andre, 56, 58
Sanders, Barry, 35, 38-39
Sanders, Deion, 18
Seifert, George, 8
Sharpe, Sterling, 29, 32, 34, 36, 43
Simmons, Wayne, 9
Smith, Chuck, 38
Smith, Emmitt, 11, 39, 48
Stallings, Gene, 20
Starr, Bart, 46
Switzer, Barry, 43
Taylor, Kitrick, 27
Teague, George, 35, 39
Unitas, Johnny, 56
Walker, Adam, 9
Wallace, Steve, 46
White, Reggie, 8, 10, 32, 33, 34, 42, 46, 60
Winder, Sammy, 16
Wolf, Ron, 21, 24, 25, 57
Woolford, Donnell, 44
Young, Steve, 7, 9, 10, 29, 46, 57

PHOTO CREDITS:
AP/Wide World Photos: 2, 8, 16, 26, 29, 30, 33, 36, 40, 45, 48, 54, 56, 59; courtesy Sea Coast Echo: 12, 15; Sports Information Department, University of Southern Mississippi: 19, 20; courtesy Atlanta Falcons: 23.

PLEASE RETURN TO
TIMOTHY CHRISTIAN SCHOOL
2008 Ethel Road
Piscataway, NJ 08854